TALES FROM
THE TURF

Happy Father's
Day '93

From Your Loving
Son
Dad

TALES FROM THE TURF

Text by Jeffrey Bernard
Illustrations by Hugh Dodd

WEIDENFELD AND NICOLSON · LONDON

Deciduous

Early one December I went down to Lambourn to see my trainer. God, how I'd longed to be able to say that. The rich owners of this world may be used to the phrase, but I got a kick out of being able to use it at last. Let me explain. In a moment of lunacy, I had invested in a part-share in a two-year-old and now here I was being driven by Doug Marks, his usual eccentric self, up to the gallops to watch my filly have a lesson in how to gallop. It was only her third outing and she was accompanied by three three-year-olds. I was quite pleased with myself for naming her Deciduous, since she was by Shiny Tenth out of Elm Leaf, but it seemed I'd given her a name which for some strange reason her trainer had great difficulty in pronouncing.

That morning we decided to settle for his calling her 'your horse'. It suited me and exaggerated the feeling of ownership. It was the first time I'd had a good look at her. She was chestnut with hardly one white hair, on the small side as would be anyone who wouldn't be two until January 1st. She had a nice intelligent head and seemed quite alert and lively. I watched her do two gallops of approximately three furlongs each and although she was very green she stayed with the three-year-olds, tucked in behind them, with something that looked amazingly like enthusiasm. Perhaps horses actually like galloping, I thought, but it looked like fearfully hard work to me.

Back in the yard Doug reminded me of how well one of his inmates had run in the Grand National the previous March until being brought down at Beecher's the second time around. I watched the video recording of the race and Doug made one of his usual 'funnies'.

'Yes,' he said, 'when I saw him still standing and going well as they passed the stands, I thought to myself, I must start feeding that horse.' Incredible as it may seem, there are a few owners thick enough to take that sort of remark seriously. They'd better stay away from Mr Marks. I remember one Newmarket sales when two Americans approached Doug and asked him if they could look at a horse he was going to sell. They were interested and wanted a good look at him before he went into the sale ring. I walked with them to the box and Doug got the lad to bring him out and walk him around. To the astonishment of the Americans and all standers-by, Doug then got hold of the lad and walked him around.

'A nice little mover,' he said. 'I picked him up for thirty bob the other day in Huddersfield. Got him from a remand school. I know he's a bit plain, but he should make up into quite a nice sort.'

Under Starter's Orders

Doug used to send me these ridiculous letters about Deciduous: 'Geoff Baxter rode her out at work this morning. She galloped so well she's bound to win a race.' I couldn't afford to own her. She was syndicated and I just had a leg, but she raced in my name and colours and I never met the other owners.

Soon, despite other events such as the One Thousand and Two Thousand Guineas, the race I was awaiting most eagerly, with bated, pastis-smelling breath, was one at Wolverhampton on Monday May 2nd, as it was to mark the first racecourse appearance of Deciduous. Geoff Baxter had been continuing to ride her in work and Doug Marks was still sending me boring business letters about the price of oats and hay, but there had been a large number of postscripts to the effect that Deciduous had been galloping really well. Trainers have a tendency to exaggerate the merits of their charges, using phrases like 'He's jumping out of his skin', and 'He can catch pigeons on the gallops'. My own favourite exaggeration is the one they use after the horse has won a race. Even if it's only got up by a neck the trainer will say, 'He won doing hand-springs.'

I travelled up to Wolverhampton from Euston with an extremely hard nut, physically that is, of a bookmaker who warned me to expect nothing of Deciduous – as if I didn't already know – and during the journey, discussing people who've gone down the drain via the Turf, he came out with what, for me, was the saying of the week. 'Yes,' he said, 'this racing game tames bleedin' tigers.'

It was the first time I'd been to Wolverhampton for some years and I'd forgotten just how underrated a track it is. Forget the town, the track is very worthwhile if ever you have the bad luck to be in that part of the world. There's a good restaurant in the Members' where you can sit and eat and drink *and* see every yard of how you're throwing your money away.

As soon as I got to the course I walked over to see Deciduous being saddled up. She was walking around the tiny paddock with the others, awaiting their various trainers, and she looked really sweet. There's something very touching about looking at two-year-olds who've never been out on a track. You know they don't really know what it's all about, and when you're personally involved you realize what a hell of a thing it is: you wonder how on earth they must feel when they see that seemingly endless stretch of gallop in front of them from the stalls. They're just big babies. Deciduous looked in very good nick and the only fault you could find was that she needed a bit more time and a bit more muscle on her arse, which is where it counts and where the propulsion comes from.

I'd been pretty sure from the day before that she wasn't going to win, since Doug Marks had written to me from Lambourn warning me that on

First Time Out

the evidence of the home gallops she didn't like soft going. Her dainty feet got stuck in too far. But if she had won and I hadn't had a penny on her I would have been furious. In the end I made a sort of compromise, not too little and certainly not too much, and had a fiver each way. In the parade ring she certainly wasn't put to shame by any of the other runners, and by the time the jockeys walked in to mount the adrenalin was fairly bubbling.

Doug told Taffy Thomas to 'Win if you can' and I went into the Ring to place my bet while they cantered down to the start. It came as something of a shock to me when I saw that Deciduous had opened at as little as 4–1 and was third favourite. Did someone know something that the connections didn't? In fact, what the hell was going on? I didn't have to wait long to find out. She started drifting and ended up being returned at 19–1.

From the off I knew she was going to get stuffed since she came out of the stalls very slowly, but it was some consolation to see my colours making some sort of headway as they came to the half-way stage. At the death she finished eighth of the fifteen runners with Thomas sitting pretty quietly on her having not knocked her about. Eighth of fifteen in the 2.15 at Wolverhampton, the Lichfield Maiden Fillies' Stakes, run over five furlongs. Those were the bare facts. But dear oh Lord, what a lot more there is to it when you're personally involved.

The Sweet Smell of Success

Final Instructions

Giving instructions to a jockey in the paddock before a race is a way that trainers like to butter up their owners, who to a large extent know absolutely nothing about racing tactics. The idea of the average owner giving the likes of Steve Donoghue, Gordon Richards or Lester Piggott instructions is quite laughable. Indeed, it is a complete waste of time, unless the horse has some strange quirk.

There was a horse who ran at Salisbury one day who was put off by the noise that other horses made, so that he would only hit the front and go hell for leather when he couldn't hear the other hooves. To achieve this his trainer put a Tampax in each of the horse's ears and told the jockey not to pull them out until a hundred yards from the winning post. It worked remarkably well until the stewards made a fuss. The horse never won again.

The first time Deciduous ran, at Wolverhampton, she was due to be ridden by Taffy Thomas. Going into the paddock to give instructions had long been one of my greatest fantasies. It turned out to be a complete anticlimax. I had expected Taffy to walk up to me, tug his forelock and address me as 'Sir'. Instead, he walked over to me and said, 'Hello, Jeff. How's it all going then?' I had forgotten that I used to spend time getting legless with some regularity in Taffy's local, the White Lion at Newmarket.

One of my favourite stories about giving instructions concerns one of our noble lords about 100 years ago. When the horse lost, it was Snowden who was blamed. He simply said: 'I'm sorry, my lord, but I couldn't come without the horse.'

Of course it's always interesting to go with a trainer into the paddock and meet the jockey and listen to the riding instructions. I remember one Saturday in August years ago when I actually got up early enough to go onto the Newmarket gallops with that excellent trainer Bill Marshall. He was then training from the Eve Lodge Stable built and now occupied by the Piggotts.

I went into the paddock with Bill to watch him saddle up The Guvnor for the fourth race. Alan Bond had the mount, and there was a fair amount of optimism in the air that in receipt of two stone from Berkeley Square The Guvnor might bring it off. 'Keep him up with the others all the time, because he loves to be in the thick of things, and then see if you can make a run for it three furlongs out.'

At that moment, Rhodomontade's jockey walked by to mount his horse and Marshall said, 'Oh shit. He heard us.' This was followed by a lot of laughing and I felt as though I was in the middle of a schoolboy conspiracy. Sadly for all the connections, The Guvnor came third and Berkeley Square lived up to his name by demonstrating a fair amount of class.

Final Instructions

The 66–1 Outsider

There's a kind of typically lucky woman owner that you see on many racecourses. She invariably wears a mink coat on her back, which is where unfriendly people say she earned it. Her name is probably either Madge or Renée and she lives in a service flat in St John's Wood. She's a widow, and if she isn't she's married to a bedridden millionaire who caters to her every whim. Although the said Renée is as hard as steel or platinum, she's surprisingly generous when it comes to standing her round in the Members' Bar, and when she does have a winner it is champagne all round.

The trainer she is talking to is probably a Yorkshireman, shrewd and on the fringe of being bent. One of this type of trainer was forced to retire when dope tests became more routine. He used to buy clapped-out horses from Newmarket which were considered to be past their peak. He would take them to his yard near Malton, give them strange things for breakfast and enter them in handicaps which he would win at quite remarkable odds. Describing this man, one Newmarket trainer told me that the tack-room in his yard resembled a chemistry laboratory. He once won the Lincoln at 25–1 with a horse that was supposed to be absolutely useless.

The Lincoln used to be a favourite race for this sort of trainer. One currently very successful trainer was once a stable lad in Newmarket. His employer went away on holiday leaving this lad in charge. It is not known what he gave the horse, but he sold every possession he had, all his wife's possessions and borrowed from every person who would lend him a dollar. He backed the horse from 66–1 down to 100–8 and it cruised in. When his boss came back he handed in his notice and opened his own establishment with the winnings.

If our Renée here had been the owner of that horse he would have been decent enough to let her in on it, trusting her not to shoot her mouth off, and both of them would have had a real touch.

There used to be a woman exactly like this one who frequented Windsor evening meetings. She was always there, and for some reason took a fancy to me on the days when I was on the *Sporting Life*, in about 1971. She always bought me plates of hot roast beef which I wish more racecourses would do, Windsor being the only one I know of – and she'd pour whisky down me and never expect anything in return, not that I was in a position to offer very much.

The 66–1 Outsider

Jockeys

Top jockeys can best be summed up as rich little men. Lester Piggott was richer and not as little as most. He was the guvnor, and now he's returned to race-riding he may prove he still is, especially on the big occasion, though Pat Eddery must be getting heartily fed up at hearing that.

I once went to Newmarket to interview Lester for the *Sunday Times*. He rode two hot-pots for a big trainer on the gallops that morning and when he got off the second one he said it was a Derby prospect. On the way back to his house we came across a loose horse that had obviously thrown its stable lad on the Heath and was now standing stupidly in the middle of the road. It was the Derby prospect. I pointed it out to Lester and suggested we stop and get hold of it – after all, it could easily have been smashed up by a car. Lester smiled rather wickedly: 'No, Jeffrey. You never catch hold of a loose horse. You can spend all bloody day hanging onto it.' I thought this a charmingly cynical approach.

At the end of the morning I explained I had to get back to Newbury for the races. 'You're an idiot,' he said, 'don't you realize I'm riding there this afternoon? You can have a lift in my aeroplane.' So we flew to Newbury in his four-seater with Geoff Wragg and another trainer. I got out at the races, said thank you very much and thought no more about it. A week later I got a bill for thirty-five quid. A little later, a reminder followed. Incensed by this display of parsimony, I told one of the stalls handlers about it. This same man found himself loading Lester into the stalls one day soon after. 'Lester,' he said, 'that thirty-five quid bill you sent to Jeffrey – he's very annoyed about it …' Apparently when the stalls opened Lester was laughing so much that he almost fell off.

Lester is astute and funny, but his humour is dry and abrasive and when teamed up with a brain that fires on all cylinders it is easily misunderstood. Most of the stories about his meanness are really about Lester winding people up – like the sweltering August day he gave Willie Carson a lift back from York. Lester told his chauffeur to pull up at a garage selling ice-cream. 'Get three,' he told the man, who returned shortly and handed over three cones to Lester. Carson put his hand out for one, but Lester simply turned to him and said: 'They're mine. Get your own.' This sort of incident, purely an experiment to see how discomfited Carson could look, has been exaggerated to make Lester seem pathologically mean, which he isn't. He's just tight.

I can remember sitting outside a café in Chantilly feeling bored and depressed and anxious about my fast-dwindling expenses – the afternoons are horribly dead in that otherwise lovely place – and who should walk by

Soft Going

but Lester. I never thought that taut, serious face would be a cheering sight off a horse but I nearly burst into a couple of verses of 'We'll Meet Again' à la Vera Lynn. But Lester didn't even stop to say hello. That might have cost him a glass of wine.

It's not true either that he never smiles, though it doesn't look as if there'd be room between the crags. I remember a day in Ascot when he landed the King George VI and Queen Elizabeth Diamond Stakes with a brilliant ride on that gutsy horse The Minstrel. He then went on to win the Brown Jack Stakes on the Queen's horse Valuation. In the enclosure afterwards he was talking to the Queen and beaming like a cat that's got the cream. I gather that the Queen had said to him: 'You made it look so easy, Lester.' And with an admirable lack of false modesty he had replied: 'It *was* easy, Ma'am.'

On another occasion Lester was booked to ride an animal trained by the sort of twit who shouldn't be allowed to look after a mule, let alone millions of pounds' worth of horseflesh. The trainer had a hefty punt on his horse, but they were beaten by a neck. He said to Lester afterwards: 'That's it, Lester. You'll never ride for me again.' Dry as you like Lester replied: 'Oh well, I'd better hang up my boots then, hadn't I?'

Soon after he was sacked by Vincent O'Brien, Lester popped up and beat one of his horses by a short head in a thrilling finish. O'Brien was standing miserably in the unsaddling enclosure. Lester walked past him on his way to the scales and gave him a huge grin. 'Will you be needing me again?' were his only words.

As in all departments, Lester Piggott talks a great deal of sense about gambling. I once told him the story of an Italian waiter in Frith Street who put his life's savings on a horse that Lester was riding and which started at 6–5. You don't back horses like that with your life's savings, not unless you're mad, but this man did, and Lester got stuffed that day – beaten by a very small margin, a neck or half a length. The waiter was reduced to hysteria and suddenly began screaming in the betting shop: 'Alla my life I givva my wife good food … My children havva the shoes on their feet … They eata well, they clothed, I paya the rent … and now this fucking bastard Piggott, he killa me, he ruin my life …' In a little while he was transferred to the Middlesex Hospital in a straitjacket. When Lester heard this story he simply remarked that people like that are idiots. And he was right. After all, no one twists your arm to have a bet. If you lose your wages, that's your fault.

Another jockey I had a great deal of admiration for was Jimmy Lindley, a genuinely nice man, and a shrewd one to boot. Jim Joel, the millionaire owner, adores him too. Lindley used to go there for dinner and drop dreadful hints. Once he said: 'By God, Mr Joel, those two Purdies are beautiful things, the best I've ever seen.'

The Jockey's Lot

'Do you really like them?' Joel replied. Then he summoned the butler and said, 'Put the Purdies down to Lindley,' talking of his will.

One weekend Lindley was at Joel's house and knew he was going to get some very good port. So he bunged the butler ten quid before dinner to tell him what the port was. When it was served up he said: 'My God, Mr Joel, this is the best port I've ever tasted.'

Joel said: 'I didn't realize you knew about port, Jimmy.'

Jimmy replied: 'Oh, I've always been very keen on port, sir, I made a little study of it.'

'What do you think this is, then, Jimmy?'

'Well I would hazard a guess and say it was Croft 1937.'

Joel was so impressed he summoned the butler again and said, 'Put the port down to Mr Lindley.'

Then Jimmy went too far one day. At the bottom of Joel's staircase was some enormous bloody statue from Tutankhamun's tomb or something. Jimmy said: 'My God, Mr Joel, I've never seen anything as wonderful as that ...'

And Joel said: 'Don't tell me you're interested in archaeology too, Jimmy, your interests are getting too widespread.' But it was a nice try, and Lindley has always had an eye for the main chance.

He also has made a great success of his post-riding life. Some jockeys do and some don't. Into the latter category, sadly, falls Barry Brogan, one of the most talented of jump jockeys since the war. I was at Huntingdon races once, where he rode two winners and I backed three. Afterwards we met in a local hotel, and after such a good day we had a riotous evening and night, which I can't remember. But what I do remember is waking up in a room in the hotel in a very large double bed, with Barry Brogan, and between us who should be lying there but the hotel charwoman. I realized what her profession was because there was a bucket and mop by the bed.

Barry disappeared fairly quickly, and I went downstairs to reception to pay my bill. The hotel manager said: 'It would be very much appreciated, sir, if you never came back to this hotel again.' I thought little of this. I'd been barred from places before, and it didn't come as too great a shock, and the way I felt told me I must have been pretty awful. But what did surprise me was the small delegation from the local council who shortly arrived at the hotel. The spokesman told me not to worry about being barred from the hotel. Instead would I and Mr Brogan do them a favour by never, ever coming back to the town of Huntingdon?

Barry was a good chap, a typically handsome Irishman, who won, among many other races, the 1971 King George VI Chase on The Dikler. But success went to his head, he gambled a lot, and eventually booze was his undoing.

One of my favourite racing jokes is actually true. It concerns an

A Fall at the Last

Australian jockey, who will have to remain nameless, who got a retainer to ride for a big stable in Chantilly. He duly arrived and they found he couldn't speak a word of French. They got an interpreter to him who said, 'Now the first thing you'll have to learn is a phrase the guvnor might use when he gives you the leg up at Longchamp tomorrow. It's *"Pas aujourd'hui"* and it means not today.'

As a final thought on jockeys, I remember once being asked to ghost the autobiography of a famous and respected English jockey. The offer was quite tempting. I went to see the jockey, now at the end of his career, and told him I'd do it if he owned up – told the truth, that is. 'Own up!' he spluttered. 'Tell the truth! You must be stark, staring bonkers! There'd be enough evidence against me by the end of Chapter One to get me warned off for life!'

I told him I wasn't interested, in that case. But I *was* interested to read the bowdlerized version when it hit the bookstands some months later. It was the usual stuff about how he had worked his way up from stable lad to great jockey, had ridden for everyone from the Queen downwards, had led an exemplary life and blameless career, and had been presented with the usual silver cigarette box on retirement by a grateful clutch of owners. Boring.

The Weighing Room

Ireland

There are things and people that can only happen in Ireland and the place is still the friendly madhouse it has always been. I once stopped a couple of nights at Waterford. I visited a golf club there and saw a painted notice at the entrance of the place that would make an English golfer turn pale with horror: 'Members are forbidden to train greyhounds on the links.'

It was wonderfully typical of the country. Inquiring about the notice I learned that the procedure was one of getting the dog you really wanted to work out to run with two others. What they do is to get someone to stand on the green and wave a handkerchief at three men holding three dogs on the tee. The men on the tee let one go and then another and when the first one's gone fifty yards they let the important dog go another fifty yards later. Apparently the third dog tries like a lunatic to catch up the other two and the gallop, as it were, brings him on a ton. When I asked the man who took me up to the place whether the other members got annoyed at this sort of activity he told me that no they didn't, they just leaned on their clubs and made rapid bets as to whether the third dog would catch the other two.

What was so Irish was that the man who introduced me to the place was a local and highly respected doctor who had been temporarily barred from my hotel for three months for breaking a chandelier in the restaurant. You could look for years, and sadly without success, to find a doctor in England like that.

After a day of backing losers, I found myself that night in Dublin with the doctor, and he came to the rescue with a financial injection. I said that I was a bit sick of racing and just wanted to go out and have a drink in those haunts where I'd drunk with the likes of Behan years before.

'A drink,' he said. 'Well, you'll be needing twenty pounds.' (This was fifteen years ago.)

'No', I said, 'a drink means about five pounds.'

'You might run into trouble,' he said and pressed twenty quid into my hand.

'And when will you be wanting it back?' I asked, slipping into Irish.

'Next year at Royal Ascot,' he replied.

Of all people who take themselves too seriously, the English racing classes ought to plead guilty, and I mean more guilty than even those in the entertainment business. Offer some criticism to a jockey, poke some fun at a trainer and the heavens open up. I was once told I was responsible for one trainer's heart attack. I had simply remarked, somewhat facetiously, that he covered the distance of ground between his yard and his local pub

An Irish Dream

at a speed reminiscent of The Tetrarch. (He should have been so well bred!) The man exploded and apparently made some remark to the effect that trainers of racehorses were due respect because they trained racehorses. Well, well. What a funny lot some of them are. Most of the genuinely funny ones are across the sea in Ireland.

Take Mick O'Toole. He once took me to the dogs in Dublin at Selhurst Park. Now, since he was in his early days a dog trainer I was more than eager that he should mark my card. He was quick to reassure me: 'You've got nothing to worry about, Jeffrey, just follow me.' My resources were limited. I was there on feeble expenses from some magazine. There were eight dog races that night and I backed everything Mick told me to. Together we backed eight consecutive losers.

He was tremendously amused by our going skint, but I found it very hard to raise a smile since I have a genuine loathing for running out of money when I'm abroad. Actually, I'm not that fond of running out of money at Harringay, Ascot or in my betting shop, but giving handouts to bookies in Ireland or the Paris-Mutuel in France is ghastly. Anyway, O'Toole whistled all the way back to the Shelbourne Hotel with me whining beside him: 'I just don't know what to do, Mick. You've screwed me up completely. I haven't got a pot to piss in.' I've never seen a man raise a float so quickly as he did. Within three minutes his pockets were running over and he saw me all right. I tried to pay him back a day or so later but he refused: 'Keep it, Jeffrey. You don't owe me anything. You're a guest in my country.' He has a lot of friends does Mr O'Toole, he puts his money where his mouth is when he has a bet and I've never known the man complain when his horses do get stuffed.

I'd very much like to take some of the pompous English trainers over to the Curragh to show them that you don't have to imitate Colonel Blimp to train horses. Con Collins is another case, and he has extraordinary ideas of what hospitality consists of. When I called in at his establishment I was shown into a sitting-room and a maid came in carrying a tray on which were poised a glass, a bottle of Scotch whisky, a bottle of Irish, a bottle of gin, a bottle of brandy and a bottle of vodka. 'Mr Collins will be with you in five minutes and he says you're to ring the bell if you need any more to drink.'

The Luckpenny

Outings

A highlight of the year used to be the Lurcher Show, which in the old days was held on Peter Walwyn's land at Seven Barrows, Lambourn. Peter was champion trainer twice in the mid-seventies, when he won the Derby with Grundy. Although I hate parties, I used to make an exception for the one they gave for the Lurcher Show. There was always a huge marquee stuffed full of smoked salmon, roast beef, champagne and all the great names of the racing world. One year I took Tom Baker, the actor, with me. I introduced him to Fred Winter. Pat Eddery filled up his glass. Lester Piggott tripped over his feet. Tom said to Peter Walwyn, a lovely man: 'Thank you very, very much for all this. It's the most amazing party I've ever been to.' Peter was not at all taken aback: 'Oh yes, well, thank you Tom ... You know, it's awfully nice to have a few friends pop in for a drink on a Sunday, isn't it?'

I was once watching when Peter's hack threw him on the gallops. Peter lost his temper and shouted at it. The next day it did it again, and Peter's fury was doubled. On the third day, it threw him again. Peter picked his bruised body off the ground and addressed the animal as though it were a person. 'I've had enough of you,' he shouted, 'your balls are coming off in the morning.'

To be castrated for not minding your Ps and Qs is a dreadful thought, isn't it? The vet in Lambourn, Frank Mahon, was a very nice Irishman I used to drink with. I was walking past his establishment one morning when he poked his head out of the yard and asked me if I'd ever seen a horse gelded, and did I want to? Well, I thought it was all part of life's experience, and I'm not squeamish, so I said yes. I must admit I didn't enjoy myself very much. Frank first gave the poor horse an enormous injection of Valium in its neck. It soon looked a bit dopey. Then he gave it a local injection in its balls. Then he pulled out a dreadful instrument that looked like a pair of outsize garden secateurs. Snip, snip, and the horse's balls fell into the straw. Then a little terrier rushed in and started eating them. Apparently this always happened, and the dog lived almost exclusively on a diet of bollocks, something it had in common with quite a few people I've come across over the years.

The Rare Breed

In The Know

There are certain exasperating types who appear to be, or more likely enjoy giving the impression of being, in the know, though it goes without saying that most tips from jockeys, owners, trainers and gamblers are worthless. But certain signposts must be followed.

I once met Fred Rimell on the morning of the 1970 Grand National in the Adelphi Hotel in Liverpool. Hung over and desperate for a drink I went to the bar, thinking, as the bolts had only just been slid back, that I'd be the first one in. But I was wrong – Fred was already sitting there, by himself, half way through a bottle of champagne. Like a fool, despite the fact that Fred had already won two Nationals, I didn't take the hint. He was either feeling desperately ill himself or was celebrating in anticipation. Later that afternoon Gay Trip bounced home at 15–1, trainer F. Rimell.

If I'm with an expert I find the safest thing to do is to keep my mouth closed so as not to make a fool of myself. In the same way that had I ever met Albert Einstein I don't think I'd have tried to chat to him about nuclear physics.

I once went down to Sandown with a girlfriend who made the interesting observation that racing people look conspiratorial, tend to talk out of the sides of their mouths and invariably look as though they're up to no good. I've got so used to them that I don't notice, but she was absolutely right. A jockey we were meeting up with that day talked to us as though he was operating a ventriloquist's dummy and it was while sitting with him that I had quite an embarrassing moment. An owner new to the racing world joined us at our table in the bar. Thinking himself a bit of a lad, he suddenly leaned forward and said to this jockey, 'I suppose you've pulled a few in your time?' This is roughly like asking a police officer, 'Taken any good bribes this week?' The amount of people in racing who don't engage brain before operating mouth sometimes seems to grow daily.

In the Know

Tips

The thing I like most about racecourse con-men is their method of approach. A man at Kempton Park once tried to get some money off me with an excellent new line in openers. 'I'm on the brink of something great,' he told me. 'Count me out,' I replied. But I liked that: the use of the words 'brink' and 'great'. It made such a nice change from the stale old approach that you should always beware of. This runs: 'I'll tell you what I'll do for you.' It's a dead give-away, since the word 'do' lets you know straightaway that you're going to be used in some way to their advantage.

Inured as I am to personal disaster, I have come to regard losing bets over the past few years as losses of bits of paper. I don't mean to sound flash by that. I just mean that I don't expect miracles but don't mind them when they come to pass. On the other hand, when I do get what I think is a genuine bit of information, then I feel bound and obliged to pass it on.

Impersonating God – giving tips, in other words – is a tricky business. I once lumbered a friend of mine, a painter of some repute, with two complete stinkers. He is a fearless gambler and I guessed he must have lost a thousand pounds on the two. I met him on the next Monday morning over coffee and he uttered not a single word of reproach. Lovely and as it should be. I ran across him once in a betting shop. I was moaning because I was down a little. 'How's it going?' he asked. 'Awful. I've just lost twenty-five quid and I'm really fed up. How about you?' 'Not so good either,' he replied. 'I've just lost two thousand seven hundred, including the tax.' It was only 2.30. There had only been two races.

But others accept losing tips with less equanimity than my painter friend. There are those who mistakenly accept the hunch as gospel. They're not Christians, just punters, and I wish to God that they'd get it right. A tip is an opinion. It might be a strong opinion – one stated with some conviction – but it's still an opinion, and if all of them were bang on target then there wouldn't be such things as horse races. Worse than tipping losers to bad losers is tipping winners to idiots and then not backing them yourself.

I was having a shave in a barber's shop one Monday morning in Old Compton Street and the man operating the cut-throat asked me what I fancied. For a moment I couldn't answer him since I'd noticed the most extraordinary thing. Instead of using tissue paper to wipe the razor after every clean sweep of the chin, he was using betting slips nicked from the local betting shop. Having digested that, I went on to say that a certain horse of Fred Winter's might oblige at a long price. Gastronomic and alcoholic events that followed prevented me from having a wager that

The Tipster

afternoon. In the evening, when I read that the horse had won at 12–1, I choked.

At one time in my life, I found myself being followed and I didn't like it. Almost every time I struck a bet with my unlicensed bookmaker in the local pub the wager was duplicated by a woman called Eva. She had a sort of faith in me that was more dumb than blind. It had started in the spring. I had called round to her flat to discuss the previous day's appalling behaviour and to borrow some money from her. She asked me if there was, by any chance, a particular nag that I fancied that day. I told her that I'd been waiting for a certain hurdler which was running that afternoon and she gave me a tenner to put on for her. That evening I presented her with a hundred pounds and it was that evening that she got the idea that winning a hundred on a horse was as easy as falling out of a taxi.

In fact, I suspect that she got the idea that winning a hundred was something that could be done on every race, never mind once a day. We had our ups and downs, did Eva and I, and that was the beginning of the best run of luck I'd had for a very long time. We took to having snacks in the Connaught and I went on making inspired guesses and, d'you know, we just couldn't go wrong.

Then came the inevitable period when I couldn't pick anything that even made the frame, never mind won. Well, nearly. But the plucky little woman still followed me. It put me in something of a quandary.

It's something that you just can't help feeling bad about. The nitty-gritty of the business is that I can't bear putting money on for someone else even when it's their wretched choice. Another thing that's unbearable is when the person has a go at you when they lose. It's unforgivable, in fact. Eva didn't do that; she was as good as gold, or in her case platinum. What she did do when she lost was bathe me in one of those looks that labradors give you after you've kicked them and which mean, 'I hope you didn't hurt your foot.' Mind you, there wasn't much I could do about it. She was hell-bent on throwing pieces of paper at the bookmaking fraternity and if one is doomed to make that kamikaze trip to Carey Street then one might as well have company.

No, what began troubling my conscience was the fact that my luck had turned again and I had two very nourishing touches on horses trained by J. Webber. On both occasions I snuck off round the corner to put the money on, having told Eva that I wasn't betting that day. I was tipped both animals and the man that gave them to me was furious that I didn't put more on. Megalomania had reared its ugly head.

Can you imagine it? The man was actually angry that his tips hadn't made me rich?

Tic-Tac Man

Punters

In my opinion the only point in betting is to earn money when you're skint. I bet because I'm greedy and don't want to work, so I need to get something for nothing. And a word of advice: ignore tips. The nearer to the horse's mouth, the worse they are.

It has been suggested that in a few hundred years' time gamblers will be forced by law to have psychiatric treatment. It's a very simple sickness, completely infantile for a start. It's also a chronic complaint that invariably lasts for life. The gambler, after all, is the one person who is completely unmoved by the experience, especially when he loses. And I do realize that some gamblers want to lose. Time and time again I've noticed that nearly all gambling reminiscences and post-mortems concern losses and not winnings. Invariably, when recollecting the past, gamblers will say: 'I'll never forget that day. I got beaten for a thousand quid by a neck and a short head.'

For some strange reason, punters have short memories when it comes to winnings. There are of course the odd exceptions that prove the rule. One of them is a man I know who is so clinically unique he should be stuffed and mounted in the Natural History Museum. In fact, this is a very real possibility.

He devoted years to the formbook with little tangible success, but as luck would have it he did a ten-bob accumulator one day and won a large sum of money. He immediately gave up his job and flew his wife and mistress to the south of Spain, where they spent a happy month fighting over him and occasionally pouring bottles of cheap wine over his head. And of course that's where it all went. To his head, I mean.

He returned to England armed with an inordinate amount of conceit, arrogance, bitterness and fifteen shillings. He'd done it once, he said, and there was no good reason why he shouldn't do it again. Every day. The last I heard of him he was working as a messenger on a tit magazine.

I once had a friend, a compulsive gambler and habitual loser, who eventually cancelled his subscription to the *Life* as it offered too much temptation. He further stated that he owed a lot of money and was being sued for the rates. 'There's one good thing about being skint, though,' he told me. 'It keeps the mind lively and generally puts one on one's toes.'

Well, of course it does. I know it's an expensive way of keeping fit but, by God, it works. There's nothing like a bailiff on the doorstep or a brief in King's Bench to keep one up to the mark. I can recommend trouble for anyone who's complacent about life. Just think of the amount of winners that the Marchioness of Tavistock would suddenly have if she were over-drawn at Hambros, or the number of successes Charles St George would

The Compulsive Gambler

chalk up if the exhaust pipe on his Bentley fell off. It doesn't bear thinking about. It's not the sort of philosophy they teach at Trinity or Magdalen, I know, but perhaps they should. If Lester's cigar had gone out and he wasn't offered a light, just think what might have happened to Sir Gordon's record. No. It's obviously the thing to do. Go skint.

I remember having a perfectly miserable day at Fontwell Park one week, backing winner after winner until I met Jack Cohen. He bought me a drink, a cup of tea, a cigar and lent me the fare home. He then told me I was a lousy good-for-nothing. Life suddenly had some sort of meaning again and it was a tremendous relief to back the last two losers. Oh yes. I shall always be grateful to him for that.

It's hard to understand why rich people still like to bet, but they do. Robert Sangster is a shrewd punter with a lot of nerve. I was having a drink with him at Newbury one September when Fred Binns walked past. Robert said, 'Oh, by the way Fred, while you're there, can I have £5000 to win Detroit in the Arc?' I asked him why he was putting five thousand pounds on his own filly to win a race that boasted prize money of a hundred and fifty thousand and would enhance her paddock value by a million or more. 'Just for interest's sake,' he replied. And I don't know whether it's true, but the Queen is reputed to have small bets on her horses. Just a tenner a time. Charles St George, a millionaire, does a yankee every Saturday.

To see a newcomer to racing getting hooked, then stumbling, then crashing, is like watching a man falling off the top of a building in slow motion. Take Antonio. Antonio was the Portuguese barman who served in the Soho pub I used to frequent. He gave the impression of being carefree, but really he was manic. His addiction to matters concerning the Turf began one day when he put fifty pence on a horse of Scobie Breasley's called Hittite Glory. The animal trotted up at 100–1 and Antonio got the idea that he could repeat the performance every day for the rest of his life. The fact that he didn't know one end of a horse from the other made things awkward for him and watching him study the midday *Evening Standard* was like watching a junkie who can't remember how a hypodermic's put together.

Anyway, someone told him I knew the odd trainer and horse, and he started asking me to mark his card for him every day. As far as Antonio went, looking back on it, it was already too late to shout a warning. I simply tried to cushion the inevitable sickening thud by giving him a few winners on the way down, but I think the results may have speeded up his descent. I started off by giving him a couple of good things each day and then astounded myself by giving him four out of four which he did in a yankee. The very next day I gave him a nourishing 32–1 double, followed by another winner the day after which cruised in at 9–1.

A Yankee

I then began to fear for his sanity although I had always thought he was suspect in the head. In two lousy weeks only, he suddenly knew it all, and one night I nearly killed him when he, like a baby trying to walk by himself for the first time, actually had the nerve to venture an opinion. 'That horse Wollow, he's no good,' he said. So crass was the remark that I can very nearly savour it now, but at the time I was tremendously tempted to jump over the counter and hit him on the head with a bottle of his own revolting Mateus Rosé. I know a teacher at St Martin's School of Art who felt much the same when one of his students told him that Rembrandt couldn't paint, and there was Antonio, only one and a half flat seasons, a yankee and a couple of doubles old, telling me that Wollow was no good. They really make me want to weep, do newcomers to racing.

I debated whether or not I should intentionally give Antonio a couple of pigs to back in the hope that it would put him off and shut him up for good, but even that harsh measure isn't as easy as it sounds. In the fifties and in the same pub I used to have a pound bet with a friend every day in which we'd try to go through the card naming a horse in every race that would *not* get placed. Time after time I thought, and we both thought, we'd done it and then some hack would get its nose in the frame at 20–1.

If only Antonio's lunacy had stopped there. It didn't. He acquired an irritating habit of telling me that the Portuguese discovered the world. Surely, I asked him the first time he said it, you mean a part of it? No. Apparently not. Before Mr Ferdinand Magellan's trip there was nothing. Worse was to come. Antonio then fell under the spell of one 'Irish' Des, a man who claimed that Lester Piggott couldn't ride racehorses. Perhaps it's a bit like what Stevenson said about marriage. Betting on a horse is a step so grave and decisive that it attracts light-headed, variable men by its very awfulness.

Allow me to refer you to a learned book on gambling, *The Psychology of Gambling* edited by John Halliday and Peter Fuller. The book is a very serious and disconcerting one and although I've always prided myself on my ability to 'own up', I realized on reading it that my owning up has always been sheer surface stuff.

For example, I never knew until I read this learned tome that I gambled because I really feel lousy about it and not only want to lose on the nags to punish myself for this blinding practice but, to rub it in further, also want to kill my father. Speaking as an anal retentive who thought that Her Majesty's Dunfermline would be outclassed in the 1977 St Leger by the likes of Alleged and the French contingent, I always put my punting down to the simple business of asking questions. My main, first and foremost question has always been: 'Is fate, God, luck and love on my side?' The second question has usually been: 'Can I win enough money on such and such a horse to enable me to avoid actual work?'

On the Nose

But I come not to knock Freud, Halliday or Fuller, for they are honourable men, although I wouldn't mind offering a shade of odds that none of them ever did or ever has had a bet. Heavens above, can you imagine the trouble Freud would have had betting? If, as I believe to be the case, Freud turned up one hour early to catch a train, then can you imagine the trouble he would have had trying to get a bet on the 3.30 while the 2.30 was still being run? Obviously he would have been an obsessive and compulsive ante-post plunger. And, like most obsessive and anally-orientated punters, he would have shown a marked tendency to knock the bookmaker.

What really gets my nanny tote is the way that clever men, intellectuals and academics get their teeth stuck into vicarious problems. Should you ever have the bad luck or spare time to go to a party of the sort given by people who live in Docklands and who write for the *Sunday Times* and then hear the subject of compulsive gambling crop up, you'll find it a racing certainty that some bright spark – usually a feature writer who earns about fifty thousand a year and whose one assignment is to take a trip to the Dordogne to find out how some celebrity cooks aubergines – is bound to mention Dostoyevsky. There'll then be a lot of wise shakings of heads and at least two people with After Eight stains on their waistcoats will knowingly murmur: 'Christ yes. Did you read "The Gambler"? Absolutely brilliant.' No one ever seems to have tumbled that what's so bloody despicable about Dostoyevsky is that he was a lousy punter. Not just bad, but really awful. You wouldn't have passed the time of day with him in a betting shop.

God forgive me for having been so glib about my Oedipal background but as I've got this far I may as well continue. As a disastrous day's punting at Newmarket never fails to rub in, results depend a little on breeding but a lot more on the luck of the draw. Take my own infamous career on the Turf. I was sired by a scenic designer who was himself by a theatrical impresario out of an actress. My dam was a singer who was by an itinerant pork butcher out of a gypsy.

Another strange example is the case of a Yorkshire-bred friend of mine. He comes from really sound stock being as he is by a dispensing chemist out of a Salvation Army contralto. Full of promise, he came to London at the outbreak of war, attempted to take the publishing world by storm and now, fifty years later, he earns a living writing pornography in the snug of a public house behind what used to be Bourne and Hollingsworth. Taking matters like these into consideration is what the Jockey Club ought to be doing. Where they say the draw has little effect they should double-check and reorganize draining in cases of slightest camber or move the running rails so as to prevent fields splitting into two groups. My Yorkshire friend and I have been running with the group on the stands side for the past forty-five years and from where I'm standing, you lot on the far side have got a ten-length advantage. And we're entering the final furlong.

A Big Winner

Bookies

I spent a day at Sandown Park once and lost money all day long on all six races. After the last race, which cleaned me out, I approached John Bank's joint and asked if he could please lend me the train fare back to Waterloo and the taxi fare home. He just motioned to his clerk to give me a bundle of money and said, with a friendly shrug, 'Have a taxi all the way.'

The bad image of bookmakers is largely outdated. These days they are pretty straightforward businessmen and with very few exceptions – like whoever doped Pinturuschio – they are decent, honest people. If they weren't they'd be out of business very quickly indeed. Victor Chandler Senior, the late-departed dear man and father of my present bookmaker Victor Chandler Junior, was a particularly decent and honest example. He owned Brighton and Walthamstow dog stadiums and came into a lot of money after the war. He'd be in the Members' Bar with his team – his clerk, his tic-tac man and what have you – and I got very discouraged, because when I used to approach him and say, 'Hello, Victor, let's have a drink,' I would hear him muttering under his breath, 'Good news, boys, here comes the lunch money.'

I once owed Victor about twenty quid, a fortune to me then and nothing to him. I'd been avoiding him for weeks. One day I saw him come into the Members' Bar at Newbury so, like an idiot, which I was, I pretended I'd dropped something and hid under the table. After about five minutes – less than that, three minutes – a hand appeared bearing an enormous whisky. Victor's face followed and met mine: 'I thought you might be thirsty. Have a drink, Jeff.'

He was a good man. One Christmas, twenty years ago, a man from his firm came round to my flat and delivered me an entire crate of Louis Roederer Crystal, and after he left I said to my then wife, 'What a marvellous man Victor is. Fancy sending me a crate of champagne of that quality.' And she quite rightly turned round and said to me: 'You bloody idiot. That crate of champagne probably cost you five thousand pounds!'

Percy Thompson, who worked for Victor, was the biggest punter in England bar none. He'd chalk up the prices on the board, write down the bets, then he'd phone another bookmaker and have ten grand on. He had one hundred thousand pounds on Tudor Minstrel to win the Derby, and he was merely a clerk.

To this day there is a picture of Sterope, the dual Cambridgeshire winner, in young Victor's office. It's there because his dad had fifty grand on it at 40–1 in 1948. That's another story that makes people like me broke.

The Bookie

When I was in hospital a few years ago Victor came to visit me, and as he left he said, 'You'll be needing a couple of bob for buying things like toothpaste and the newspaper in the morning.' He then shoved a hundred quid under my pillow, which goes to show there are such things as generous bookmakers.

And while on the subject of gambling and hospitals, there's the time when I was sent to a very old establishment in Surrey which is like a punters' research clinic. I lay in bed trembling for a day or two and, when I came to, a nurse told me I'd been raving and saying things like 'I'll take evens.' 'Did I ask for my wife?' I enquired. 'No. But you did ask for the *Life*.'

In the next bed there was an Irishman who told me that he'd been psychologically unable to work for ten years. 'At one point,' he informed me, 'the mention of the word "work" made me feel physically sick.' The psychiatrist in the place was Irish too. On the third day of my confinement, he came along and sat down beside my bed with a great wad of papers, an instrument for measuring blood pressure, a thermometer and a midday newspaper. I thought he was going to ask me the story of my life, but not a bit of it. He went straight to the point: 'Do you think Tiernascragh can beat Phaestus?' I had a look at the weights and told him no. 'You really are in a bad way,' he told me, and left to back Tiernascragh and thus prove I was mad.

When he came back he told me he'd won on the horse of his choice, but that he'd had a saver on Phaestus just in case I happened to know what I was talking about. As he left the room he remarked, 'We had a journalist in here once who was so good at tipping that we kept him in for five months.'

My own career as a bookmaker was confined to the premises of the Coach and Horses. I had a whole queue of clients approaching me every day wanting silly little one-pound and two-pound bets. After a while I found that these small bets paid for small rounds of drinks. I wasn't aware of the fact that Customs and Excise and VAT people and even the CID had been watching me for some time. In my defence when I was arrested and taken to court my QC, a charming man who acted for me without charging me, quite rightly told the magistrate that since I'd been watched for so long and that since the police had taken so much time and also had placed bets with me, they were *agents provocateurs*. Here is the account of one David Bailey, Officer of Customs and Excise:

'On 13 June 1986 at approximately 14.00 hours I entered the Coach & Horses Public House, Greek Street, London W1. A television set was switched on showing racing from Sandown and York. A man, who I now know to be Jeffrey Bernard said, "Does anyone want anything on this?", just as the 3.00 race from Sandown was starting … [20 June 1986] After

The Sporting Life

the 2.45 race at Newmarket, Jeffrey Bernard handed coins to a woman. A man addressed as Alan on a previous visit to the premises asked Mr Bernard 'Did anyone have it?' Mr Bernard pointed to the woman to whom he had just handed the coins. During the build-up to the 3.05 race, the Irish Sweeps Derby, Jeffrey Bernard said to a man, "Dino (or Tino), do you want a bet?"

'I asked a man at the bar for the running number of a horse called Bonhomie. He consulted his newspaper and replied. At this point Mr Bernard said to me, "Do you want a bet?" I handed him two £1 coins and asked for Bonhomie. Two other customers handed Mr Bernard coins and both asked for Bonhomie. Mr Bernard said to a female companion, "I'm fucked if Bonhomie wins." Bonhomie lost and I left the premises at approximately 15.18 hours.'

God knows what the surveillance cost the taxpayer. I hate to think.

The Numbers Clerk

Gamblers

The next time you go to the races resist the temptation to dive straight into the business of losing money for a few minutes and watch the various sorts of punters as they go about their business. There are eight types that I know of:

1. *The really big punter* is the one I most like to watch. He gambles vast sums and win or lose he looks incredibly bored with the whole proceedings. The braver bookies twitch nervously as he approaches, their brains rehearsing odds and fizzing with calculations in case he has a bet with them. He'll risk five grand in just the same voice as he'll order a cup of tea.

2. *Rich idiot*, I call him. A successful businessman who likes to gamble, but whose main motivation is to impress the young girl he happens to be with. The girls with type two, incidentally, are either models, someone else's daughter, actresses, 'in showbusiness' or on holiday from Kenya. That's to say, amateur brasses. He'll always tell anyone who can be bothered to listen that he's very well up on the day.

3. *The non-punter*. He wanders round the paddock sucking thoughtfully on a cigar someone gave him pretending that he's trying to make up his mind which horse to bet on. In fact he's not going to bet on any of them. He imagines he might be mistaken for a wealthy and knowledgeable punter, or even an owner. On Monday morning he'll tell the receptionist at the second-hand car showroom where he works that he had a 'fair afternoon – not much, just a few hundred up'. She won't believe him, but won't bother to tell him so, either. He owes two weeks' rent.

4. *The compulsive punter* is usually to be found in the Members' Bar, sweating, shouting, losing badly or winning as though it's his divine right. Very unsociable, impatient and intolerant of others, he indulges in boring post-mortems after the last race when everyone else is going home and his girlfriend has just left with type two.

5. *Women gamblers*. Your average one is probably between forty and fifty although she has the constantly twitching but well-manicured hands of a a woman of sixty. She chain-smokes, uses too much perfume, wears too much jewellery and covers herself to an absurd extent with each-way bets. Don't try to talk to her. She'll think you're trying to pick her up. If you are, you'll have to earn every penny of it, and she knows all about gigolos. Her husband left her a million and she smiled all the way to the funeral, and now she's the sort of woman who has lunch alone at the Ritz. She's also a shrewd nut and probably wins in the long run.

Looking for a Winner

6. *Young gamblers.* Japanese students, Iranian remittance men, boys between public school and work, and boys between rich aunts and a carpet in Wandsworth comprise this tiresome lot. There is admittedly the odd deb's delight or a redundant Rajah who finds the 2.30 at Kempton the nearest he can get to pig-sticking, but they're mostly amateur students. They haven't a quarter the amount of money they give the impression of having and they've seen someone win in the movies so they think they can. They're suckers for tips and think they can make a fortune backing favourites. They tend to pass out in the Gents, lose their girlfriends to types one, two, three and four and are usually going to see their probation officers when they say they're going to Fortnum's.

7. *I don't like to talk about this lot. I'm one of them.* They're simply out of their depth. They know they can't win, but they'll risk it 'just this once'. They bet beyond their means, go mad when they win and cry all the way home on the train when they lose. Their cup doth not run over and there's a nasty tendency towards bitterness which takes the form of swearing in the Gents when it's empty. They also retreat there to have a private roll-call of their rapidly dwindling wad from time to time. They gamble while under the influence of alcohol and/or the astrological columns and they're even mad enough to gamble to 'get out of trouble'. That's why they're always in it. Like most dogs they have their day. About once in a lifetime.

8. *Losers.* Losing is written right across the faces of some people, and it's hard to define. There's a slightly watery look about the eye and a tendency towards ash on the waistcoat or chipped nail varnish depending on the sex. There's a nervous twitch of the lips that promises to be a brave smile or the harbinger of tears – you can never tell which. There's the touching gesture of bravado in the form of the nonchalantly produced wallet that contains one last tenner. There's a seemingly wise and knowing nod of the head which is really the burden of remorse. There's *Raceform* on the table at home with the last three weeks' installments missing. There's the old and faded trilby and the hired binoculars and the cigarettes plucked from packets of ten. At 6 pm when they return to their dreadful little flat in Tooting even the cat knows they've lost. On Monday at the office the clerk spots them looking at the day's runners at Southwell and Bangor. There's a Luncheon Voucher for lunch and then an afternoon of wishful thinking to be got through.

After that, it's gin and tonic time. Things don't seem so bad after all. Now's the time to flash the teeth in a brave smile and afford the big spender all the sympathetic laughter you can muster. You too can be a big spender. It's nearly payday and you're due for a run of luck. Saturday could be the day. Just one brave bet at 20–1 could swing it. Just one more selling-plater that stays the course. And may God have mercy on our souls.

The Winning Post

Ascot

Like most punters successful and unsuccessful I ride my races from the stands, a safer occupation than hurtling over water jumps at forty miles an hour, and an excellent place from which to criticize the endeavours of others. There is a kind of pattern to my day at the racecourse. Let's take Ascot on a big jumping day.

The poshest racecourse in England, Ascot has an extraordinary grand-stand. As far as I'm concerned it's a multi-million-pound concrete shambles. Today I meet at least six people who have got lost in it. The escalators make it seem like something between an air terminal and a modern hospital. Come to that, I suppose it's a bit like a large store with no goods. Anyway, that's not my main beef. Neither is the fact that there are more bars in the grandstand than there are pubs in Brighton.

What I can't stand about the place is that it's so bloody hard to win money there. Today, the horse that is cracked up by so many as being the star of Martin Pipe's stable is not only returned at an unbackably short price, but it gets well and truly outstayed by a rival. By the time my fancy in the second race is beaten I am making full use of the bar facilities in that dreadful stand. It is then that An Owner comes to my rescue. He is an East Ender who has already done pretty well for himself, well enough anyway to send his son to a posh prep school. When he went to watch him run in the hundred yards, or whatever they call it now, he suddenly heard to his horror his own voice screaming out, 'Come on my son!' A dead giveaway if ever there was one. He even manages to make me laugh when the wrong horse wins the big race. By this time I'm thinking of taking a part-time job, but I still don't realize that I am about to lose more than I have ever lost in a day's racing.

Meanwhile, The Owner carries on laughing at his own jokes and when someone picks him up on it he says with incredible logic, 'I laugh at my own jokes because it's the first time I've heard them.' By now I am falling for that silly old thing of picking prices and not horses, and by backing to get out of trouble I am getting deeper into it.

I had arrived at Ascot in the first place determined to back one particular horse. Now The Owner puts me off it, and it is all his fault. Another runner can't be beaten, he says, and I go along with him especially since it is a better price. What folly, what insanity. I am now breaking into the weekend money, having done the housekeeping money after losing the gas and light money. With one race to go The Owner is still laughing – I think his pockets must have been deeper than mine – and I am near to tears. Martin Pipe's representative for the last race is a certainty. Everyone knows that.

Ascot Hats

So it is the second horse of the day to start at an unbackable price. Of course, what I should have done was to shovel everything on, float a quick loan and bang that on too. But off I go, looking for outsiders again … It's a funny thing that it never occurs to one, when one's having a nervous breakdown that is, that outsiders are outsiders because they're not very good. So I back everything in the race that is more than 6–1.

I can't even bring myself to watch it. I stand on a balcony and take the occasional peep round the corner while hoping that the racecourse commentator has got his colours confused. But, damn it, the last peep I take reveals the unmistakable colours of the favourite zooming across the finishing line like Ribot. By now it is getting dark. The champagne is running out and a sausage roll left over from some other meeting is playing havoc with my guts. The girl I am with is looking at me with more disbelief than pity. I make the usual futile remarks about Monday being another day and The Owner points out quite rightly that so is Tuesday.

Switching to large ports to fend off the evening air and general angst, we stay in the bar until the course is almost deserted. I sit there uttering the usual clichés about racing teaching one to lose. Suddenly, for the life of me, I can't see what's so good about learning to lose.

The Winners' Enclosure

In the Bolly Tent

Though Cheltenham is without doubt the guvnor jump course in the world, I swear I'll never attend the Cheltenham Festival meeting again. The weather is always appalling and it is impossible to get to the bar when surrounded by five thousand Irishmen also hell-bent on getting a drink. Having said that, I remember at least two Gold Cup days when I was treated to the best hospitality that I've ever encountered on a racetrack.

That was when the present Senior Steward of the Jockey Club, Lord Hartington, known as 'Stoker', invited me into the Turf Club tent. Unfortunately both occasions were somewhat marred. On my first visit I was knocked to the drink-sodden ground by the Naked Civil Elephant Man, John Hurt, and everyone immediately assumed I was drunk, which was only partially true. On another, Geoffrey Wheatcroft, of *Daily Telegraph* and *Spectator* fame, was seen to be resting parallel to the ground supported only by two crates of tonic water. Neither his feet nor head, overlapping the boxes, were touching the ground, so that it looked like an act of levitation. Henceforth he was always known as The Rigid Man of Cheltenham, sounding like some great discovery resulting from an archaeological dig, like Piltdown Man.

It's tremendously difficult to remove someone who's completely rigid, so we had to leave him to make his own natural and somewhat lengthy recovery. Now what I like about racing people is that it's typical of them that they took hardly any notice of the event at all. I mean, imagine that scene at something like the Chelsea Flower Show. There'd be considerable tut-tutting. At Cheltenham they just said:

'What's the matter with him?'

'He's passed out.'

'Really? Have another gin.'

In the Bolly Tent

Sizing Up a Filly

Though I say myself that I have a fairly good eye for a pretty woman, I do not claim to be an expert at sizing up a horse. I once stayed the weekend with the celebrated Irish trainer Mick O'Toole at the Curragh. They are two days I shall never forget, though I can't remember them. He showed me around his yard on the morning I arrived. Being knowledgeable about horses on appearance is something you have to be brought up to, but on this occasion I was pretending, showing off. Mike pulled a horse out of a box and said, 'There's a nice little filly here we've got.'

'She looks very good,' I replied. 'She looks as though she should stay three miles in time.'

Mick's retort was to the point. 'Jesus, Jeffrey, you're a fool. She couldn't stay bloody two miles in a fucking horsebox!'

Sizing up women is an altogether easier and more enjoyable task, though racing people apply the same criteria. Indeed, I have always been fascinated by the way – and it's simply a habit, not an insult – they refer to women as though they are horses. I remember once asking Fred Winter what he thought of a certain trainer's mistress and he replied, 'Oh, she's very moderate.' Another trainer I once spoke to described a woman as being 'of little account'. I suppose the best sort of woman to spend a day at the races with would be described by Mr Winter and his colleagues as 'promising, useful, scope.'

This business of women and horses reminds me of Roger Mortimer's theory that a stallion needs to be something of a shit to be a success at stud. He even predicted to me that Mill Reef would be better than Brigadier Gerard because he was nastier, and he was absolutely right. He told me that the great racehorse The Tetrarch was very sweet-natured and found sex a most fearful bore. He only got a hundred and twenty foals, eighty of which won. When he covered a mare, apparently they had to keep dead quiet because if he heard someone sawing a piece of wood or drop a bucket, it put him right off. St Simon, on the other hand, who was a bit of a bastard and would eat a groom for breakfast, got five hundred and fifty foals. It reminds me of that great stallion Hyperion, who had an odd idiosyncrasy for a horse. He was very soft in his old age and for some reason was fascinated by aeroplanes. He would stop in the middle of covering a mare to watch one fly overhead and then resume when it disappeared over the horizon.

Sizing Up a Filly

The Members' Bar

The Members' Bar on racecourses was my downfall in 1971 because when I wrote the twice-weekly column for the *Sporting Life* it had my photograph at the top of the column and people began to recognize me as the column caught on. Quite a lot of strangers used to come up to me in the Members', and say, 'Oh, I like your column so much. Please accept this bottle of champagne, and have a large whisky with me.' Which you could hardly refuse. Well, I could hardly refuse because it slightly went to my head. It was very childish of me. Two things that don't go together, like eggs and bacon, are champagne and whisky, and I collapsed a couple of times as a result of this. One day, owing to my bad behaviour, which wasn't really bad – it simply consisted of falling asleep at a table in a Members' Bar at Ascot – the authorities at that racecourse wrote to the editor of the *Sporting Life*: 'Would your correspondent Jeffrey Bernard please not come here again.' I seem to remember that that day, because of the combination of champagne and whisky, and the fact that I'd taken a sleeping pill the night before, I was sick into a bed of geraniums beneath the Royal Box. I think She was there, because I noted for the next few months, that if ever we passed each other in the enclosure Her Majesty gave me very strange, quizzical looks. At the time, I was told, the first thing she read in the morning was the *Sporting Life* and my column, and then the *Financial Times*. So at least it can be said of Her Majesty that she has her priorities right.

The Members' Bar

A Windfall

One of my favourite bookies was the late Tommy Turner, who used to stand up on the rails for William Hill in the old days. Tommy was typical of the older generation of racing professionals. Under his soft brown hat there was a face as ripe as a windfall. I once saw him make a book at Worcester while at the same time, between races, he managed to consume an entire bottle of Courvoisier in the Members' Bar. I hasten to add it was an accurate book which showed the old firm a profit. It was Tommy who once told me that there was a pub inside the cemetery grounds at Worcester, which made it a very short journey if you weren't feeling up to scratch.

Ready for the Off

First published in 1991 by
George Weidenfeld & Nicolson Limited
91 Clapham High Street, London SW4 7TA

The author and publishers are glad to acknowledge
the *Spectator* and the *Sporting Life*, in which some of
this material originally appeared.

British Library Cataloguing in Publication Data
applied for

ISBN 0 297 81164 9

Printed in Great Britain by Butler & Tanner Ltd
Frome and London